Miss Bindergarten's Kindergarten Tales

by **JOSEPH SLATE**

illustrated by **ASHLEY WOLFF**

Dutton Children's Books · New York

Originally published as
Miss Bindergarten Has a Wild Day in Kindergarten,
978-0-525-47084-7
and Miss Bindergarten Takes a Field Trip,
978-0-525-46710-6

Published in the United States by Dutton Children's Books,
a division of Penguin Young Readers Group
345 Hudson Street, New York, New York 10014

Special Markets ISBN 978-0-525-42169-6

This 2008 edition created exclusively for Barnes & Noble Inc. under
ISBN 13: 978-1-4351-1221-6

Manufactured in China

1 3 5 7 9 10 8 6 4 2

Miss Bindergarten Has a WILD DAY in Kindergarten

Christopher says he has to go—
he really cannot wait.

Miss Bindergarten begins

a wild day in kindergarten.

Danny tends his droopy beans.

Emily spies some ants.

Franny lifts her dress and shouts,
"I love my fancy pants!"

Miss Bindergarten has

a wild day in kindergarten.

Gwen falls off the step stool.

Henry just won't share.

Ian sadly tells Miss B,
"We didn't mean to tear."

Miss Bindergarten and the librarian

have a wild day in kindergarten.

Jessie drops the bug jar.

Kiki cuts her thumb.
Lenny says, "Uh-oh, Miss B,
we need the nurse to come."

Miss Bindergarten and the nurse

have a wild day in kindergarten.

Matty checks a chrysalis.

Noah drops his rock.

Ophelia's oozy painting
is sticking to her smock.

Patricia trips and flips her tray.

Quentin overloads.

Raffie Mack soaks **S**ara when his apple juice explodes.

Miss Bindergarten and the cafeteria helper

have a wild day in kindergarten.

Tommy dumps in
too much dirt.

Ursula's seed pack rips.

Vicky pours in waaaaaaay too much, and the cardboard carton drips.

Now Miss Bindergarten and the custodian

have a wild day in kindergarten.

Wanda whacks the principal.

Xavier skins his knee.

Yolanda says, "Come look, Miss B!"

Zach set the butterflies free."

Miss Bindergarten and everyone enjoy

an even wilder day in kindergarten.

"**S**ometimes even a wild day," says Miss B, "turns up something wonderful to see."

Life cycle of a PLANT

Adam · Alligator

Brenda · Beaver

Christopher · Cat

Danny · Dog

Emily · Elephant

Franny · Frog

Gwen · Gorilla

Henry · Hippopotamus

Ian · Iguana

Jessie · Jaguar

Kiki · Kangaroo

Lenny · Lion

Matty · Moose

Noah · Newt

Miss Bindergarten's
WILD DAY
Kindergarten

Ophelia · Otter

Patricia · Pig

Quentin · Quokka

Raffie · Rhinoceros

Sara · Squirrel

Tommy · Tiger

Ursula · Uakari monkey

Vicky · Vole

Wanda · Wolf

Xavier · Xenosaurus

Yolanda · Yak

Zach · Zebra

CoCo · Cockatoo

Miss Bindergarten
Border collie

Mrs. Simpson
Suricate

Mr. King
Penguin

Mrs. Leo
Leopard

Nurse Nelson
Nyala

Ms. Chavez
Chimpanzee

Carl Cox
Coyote

Miss Bindergarten Takes a Field Trip with Kindergarten

Today is field trip day. . . .

FIELD
TRIP
DAY

circle

LOOK
for these
SHAPES!

diamond

rectangle

star

FIELD TRIP

Adam's dad's a chaperone.

Brenda's mom is, too.

Christopher says,
"Hey, don't leave yet—
a stone hopped
in my shoe."

Miss Bindergarten goes to the

bakery with kindergarten.

Danny cuts some cookies out.

Emily sees them bake.

Franny squirts pink icing
on a scrumptious
chocolate cake.

Now Miss Bindergarten goes to the

fire station with kindergarten.

Gwen McGunny rings a bell.

Henry holds a hose.

Ian makes a funny face
and laughs as his nose grooOWS.

Jessie learns
Stop, Drop, and Roll.

Kiki tries
on gear.

Miss Bindergarten slides down the pole, and Lenny gives a cheer.

Now Miss Bindergarten goes to the

post office with kindergarten.

Matty picks the planet stamps.

Noah taps the locks.

Ophelia asks where letters go when you slide them through the slots.

Patricia steers
a canvas cart.

Quentin checks
the scale.

"Mrs. Wong," **R**affie asks, "is it fun to push the mail?"

Now Miss Bindergarten goes to the

library with kindergarten.

Sara grabs her favorite chair.

Tommy hugs a book.

Mr. Mack clicks the mouse.
"Here, **U**rsula, take a look!"

Vicky likes hot-air balloons.

Wanda loves the ships.

"A book is like a ticket to all sorts of splendid trips."

Now Miss Bindergarten goes to the

park with kindergarten.

Xavier shouts,
"Where's Brenda's mom?"

Yolanda looks behind her.

"Don't worry. She's not lost," says **Z**ach.
"I know where we can find her."

Now Miss Bindergarten goes—whoa!

stops!—with kindergarten.

Adam's dad sets out the cups.

Brenda's mom pours punch.

Miss Bindergarten cuts the cake...

. . . and they all sit down

to munch!

Did you see these shapes?

we saw these shapes at the bakery

we saw these shapes at the fire station

circle

square

rectangle

triangle

diamond